Welcome to ALADDIN QUIX!

If you are looking for fast, fun-to-read stories with colorful characters, lots of kid-friendly humor, easy-to-follow action, entertaining story lines, and lively illustrations, then **ALADDIN QUIX** is for you!

But wait, there's more!

If you're also looking for stories with tables of contents; word lists; about-the-book questions; 64, 80, or 96 pages; short chapters; short paragraphs; and large fonts, then **ALADDIN QUIX** is *definitely* for you!

ALADDIN QUIX: The next step between ready to reads and longer, more challenging chapter books, for readers five to eight years old.

Read more ALADDIN QUIX books!

By Stephanie Calmenson

Our Principal Is a Frog!
Our Principal Is a Wolf!
Our Principal's in His Underwear!
Our Principal Breaks a Spell!
Our Principal's Wacky Wishes!

Royal Sweets
By Helen Perelman

Book 1: *A Royal Rescue*
Book 2: *Sugar Secrets*
Book 3: *Stolen Jewels*
Book 4: *The Marshmallow Ghost*
Book 5: *Chocolate Challenge*

A Miss Mallard Mystery
By Robert Quackenbush

Dig to Disaster
Texas Trail to Calamity
Express Train to Trouble
Stairway to Doom
Bicycle to Treachery
Gondola to Danger
Surfboard to Peril
Taxi to Intrigue

Little Goddess Girls
By Joan Holub and Suzanne Williams

Book 1: *Athena & the Magic Land*
Book 2: *Persephone & the Giant Flowers*
Book 3: *Aphrodite & the Gold Apple*
Book 4: *Artemis & the Awesome Animals*

Little GODDESS Girls

Athena & the Island Enchantress

JOAN HOLUB & SUZANNE WILLIAMS

ALADDIN QUIX

New York London Toronto Sydney New Delhi

ALADDIN QUIX
Simon & Schuster Children's Publishing Division
1230 Avenue of the Americas, New York, New York 10020
First Aladdin QUIX paperback edition August 2020
Text copyright © 2020 by Joan Holub and Suzanne Williams
Illustrations copyright © 2020 by Yuyi Chen
Also available in an Aladdin QUIX hardcover edition.
All rights reserved, including the right of reproduction in whole or in part in any form.
ALADDIN and the related marks and colophon are trademarks of Simon & Schuster, Inc.
For information about special discounts for bulk purchases,
please contact Simon & Schuster Special Sales at 1-866-506-1949
or business@simonandschuster.com.
The Simon & Schuster Speakers Bureau can bring authors to your live event. For more
information or to book an event contact the Simon & Schuster Speakers Bureau
at 1-866-248-3049 or visit our website at www.simonspeakers.com.
Designed by Tiara Iandiorio
The illustrations for this book were rendered digitally.
The text of this book was set in Archer Medium.
Manufactured in the United States of America 0720 OFF
2 4 6 8 10 9 7 5 3 1
Library of Congress Control Number 2020935790
ISBN 978-1-5344-7959-3 (hc)
ISBN 978-1-5344-7958-6 (pbk)
ISBN 978-15344-7960-9 (eBook)

Cast of Characters

Oliver (AH•liv•er): Athena's puppy

Hestia (HESS•tee•uh): A small, winged Greek goddess who helps Athena and her friends

Owlie (OWL•ee): A talking owl in magical Mount Olympus

Yellow Wing (YEH•low WING): The Owlie who travels to the island to help Athena find and free Heracles

Heracles (HAIR•uh•kleez): A strong boy with dark, curly hair who carries a big, bumpy club

Hydras (HI•druhz): Huge snakelike sea monsters with multiple heads

Circe (SUR•see): A beautiful but vain enchantress who lives on an island

Medusa (meh•DOO•suh): A mean mortal girl with snakes for hair whose stare can zap mortals to stone

Zeus (ZOOSS): Most powerful of the Greek gods who lives in Sparkle City and can grant wishes

Hephaestus (heh•FESS•tuss): An evil king who lives under a mountain on an island

Contents

Chapter 1: The Boat — 1

Chapter 2: A Big Black Key — 8

Chapter 3: Heracles — 22

Chapter 4: Visitors — 45

Chapter 5: The Big Rescue — 53

Chapter 6: A Battle — 63

Word List — 83

Questions — 85

Authors' Note — 87

The Boat

Eight-year-old Athena bent over the toy boat she'd made months ago for a science project. When her long brown hair fell across her face, she pushed it back.

"Blow, wind, blow. Go, ship, go.

Sail away, across the bay," she chanted. But her magic spell didn't work. Her boat just sat in the water. **Sigh.** She was actually very good at making things. Besides the boat, she'd made a cute clay pot in art class and a wooden flute in music. But her spells only seemed to work on **Mount Olympus**.

Athena had returned home from some exciting adventures in that magic land just one week ago. There, at the tip-top of the mountain in Sparkle City, she had learned she was a **goddess**!

She'd been glad to get back home. She liked school and her other activities. Still, another adventure would be fun! She missed Persephone, Aphrodite, and Artemis. They were the goddess girl friends she had made on Mount Olympus.

Maybe most of all she missed her cute little dog, **Oliver**. She'd always wanted a real dog. And he'd become her pet there. Sadly, she'd had to leave him behind when she came home. Artemis, who loved animals, was taking care of him until Athena returned to Mount Olympus.

Just then, a voice called to her. "Come back, Athena! We need your help . . . on a quest!" She knew that voice. It was **Hestia**, a tiny winged goddess from Mount Olympus!

"Hestia?" Athena looked around, but didn't see her. No matter. Hestia had told her how to get back to the magic land. And she wanted to go.

She was needed, after all! But on a quest? What could that mean?

She looked at the golden sandals on her feet. Each had a white wing at the heel. She clicked both heels together like Hestia had told her, and said:

"Magic sandals, whisk me high.
To Mount Olympus, I will fly."

Right away, a strong wind whipped up over the bay. It turned her little boat in circles. The boat was growing larger. **Wait! No!** Athena was growing smaller! White-capped waves crashed onshore. One swept up. It tumbled her into the boat. She had shrunk so small that she fit inside it!

Athena clung to the sides of her boat. She felt dizzy as the waves whirled it round and round. It was like she was in a rainstorm spinning down a bathtub drain! That was her very last thought before the boat came to a stop. **_Thunk!_**

2

A Big Black Key

The boat landed on a sandy white beach. Athena leaped out. As her feet touched ground, she grew to her right size again. She bent to pick up the tiny boat, but just then a wave caught it.

"Oh no!" she cried out as it was carried away.

She looked around. She seemed to be on an island. "Hello?" she called. No one answered.

Beyond the island's beach she saw houses and hills. And even a mountain. But it didn't look anything like Mount Olympus. She headed toward the houses. Maybe she could find someone who could help her find Hestia. And her friends, too.

As she walked, she knocked

on doors. "Anybody home?" she called again and again. No one answered.

Suddenly she heard a hoot. A cute yellow owl swooped down from a rooftop. It was an **Owlie!** Athena had met three of the talking owls in her last Mount Olympus adventure.

"Yellow Wing!" Athena called out, smiling. "I'm back! I got a call for help from Hestia. Can you help me find her?"

But the Owlie couldn't reply

right away. Because it had a big black key in its beak. It dropped the key at her feet.

Athena picked it up. A white ribbon printed with two words was looped through it. The words were: HELP **HERACLES**. She frowned. "What's a Heracles?"

"I'll explain later," said Yellow Wing. **"Follow me!"** Without another word, the Owlie flew off toward the hills.

"Wait up!" Athena looped the ribbon with the key around her neck. She raced after the yellow owl.

After passing more houses, they reached the first hill. They entered a forest and came to a lake. Beside the lake was a sign.

"'Beware of **Hydras**,'" Athena read aloud. "What's a Hydra?" she asked Yellow Wing. "And you never told me what a Heracles was either."

Before Yellow Wing could

answer, the lake began to churn. *Splash! Splash! Splash!* Three sea monsters popped up! A green one with thirteen heads, a purple one with ten heads, and a red one with five heads.

"SSSSS!" they hissed.

Athena gasped. "Those are the biggest snakes I've ever seen!"

The sea monsters heard her. They flicked their forked tongues. **"HISSS!** We are not sssnakes. We are Hydrasss. How dare you bother us!" they called out.

Yellow Wing flew to land on top of the sign. "Those are Hydras, all right," it said to Athena. "And Heracles is a boy Hestia wants us to find."

Athena nodded. "Hey! Do you know where to find a boy named Heracles?" she called out to the monsters.

"HISSS!" Ignoring her question, the Hydras began gliding closer. **"Run away!"** Yellow Wing screeched to Athena. Then it flew off.

"G-good idea!" She took off too.

The Hydras were almost to the shore now. "You can't essscape usss!" the green Hydra called out. It flicked all thirteen of its tongues.

"Um," Athena called to Yellow Wing. "Can Hydras walk on land?"

The red Hydra answered. "No, but we can **slither** on land!"

"Dibsss on the girl!" the purple Hydra yelled. "She will make a tasssty sssnack!"

"No fair!" the green Hydra roared. "I've got more mouthsss

to feed than you! She'sss mine!"

Athena shivered. Hestia, the tiny goddess, wanted her to help Heracles. But how could she do that if a Hydra gobbled her down! But wait. Athena was a goddess too. And she had magic sandals that could help her escape!

"Fly, sandals, fly. Take me up to the sky!" she chanted. Nothing happened. The wings at each heel didn't flap. Why weren't her sandals working on this island? **"Oh no!"** she cried. "My boat is gone and my sandals' magic isn't working. How will I ever get back home?"

"We've got other things to worry about right now!" called Yellow Wing. "Like Hydras!"

By now the three monsters had reached shore. Leaving the lake, they slithered after Athena and Yellow Wing.

"You two can share the bird!" the thirteen-headed green Hydra yelled to the red and purple ones.

"No! I don't like feathersss," the

purple Hydra's ten heads hissed. "They get ssstuck in my teeth."

"You two are ssso ssselfish!" hissed the red Hydra. "I should get them both. Ssso I can get ssstronger and grow more headsss!"

"Nonsssenssse!" the green Hydra hissed. It whipped its tail out and smacked all five of the red Hydra's heads. *SMACK! SMACK! SMACK! SMACK! SMACK!* **"OW! OW! OW! OW! OW!"** the heads yelled, one after the other.

Then all the Hydra-heads started calling one another names and smacking one another with their tails. They forgot all about Athena and Yellow Wing.

Phew! thought Athena. Quietly, she and Yellow Wing sneaked away.

Just over the top of that first hill, they came to a small shed with a locked door. "Quick. Try the key!" said Yellow Wing.

Athena poked the large black key in the lock. "It fits!" She turned

the key. **Creeeak!** The door
opened. She gasped when she saw
what was inside.

3

Heracles

A boy with dark, curly hair was asleep on the stone floor! He was hugging a bumpy club the size of an extra-extra-large baseball bat in his arms like a favorite teddy bear. And there was a padlocked chain of thick metal links wound around him!

"Hey, are you Heracles?" Athena whispered to him. "Wake up." But the boy slept on.

Yellow Wing lifted the chain in its beak, then let it fall. "I wonder if this has magic that's keeping him asleep."

"Hmm. Maybe this key will work in that padlock, too," said Athena. **Click.** The key worked. When the chain fell away, the boy woke up! He blinked when he saw Athena and Yellow Wing. "Who are you?"

"I'm Athena. We just set you free," she explained.

"I'm Yellow Wing," said the Owlie. "Are you Heracles?"

"Yup," said the boy. "The goddess Hestia sent me on a quest to free the queen, who is the rightful ruler of this island. She was captured by an evil king who took over to rule in her place. Everyone is afraid of him and his evil magic. They're all hiding."

So that's why no one had answered when I'd knocked on doors, thought Athena.

"The king locked me up in here. I've got to go." Jumping up, Heracles ran out of the shed. Athena and Yellow Wing followed as he went downhill.

"**Wait!** Hestia sent me, too,"

Athena told him. "Maybe I'm supposed to help you rescue this queen."

Heracles slowed some, but he didn't stop. "Thanks, but I don't need your help. I'm on my way to ask an **enchantress** named **Circe** to come with me. That'll probably be enough help."

Athena walked beside him. "So the king stopped you before you could see her?"

"Yeah." As they walked, Heracles began to twirl his club over his head like a baton. "He's got spies everywhere. Someone must have told him I was coming. He cast a spell on me and locked me up."

That club looks super heavy, thought Athena. *Heracles must be really strong!* But she needed to get him to let her help.

Yellow Wing flew down to sit on her shoulder. "Athena should go with you," the Owlie told Heracles, as if it had read her mind.

He stopped twirling. "Why?"

"She's pretty smart." Yellow

Wing said. "You've probably heard of the evil snake-haired **Medusa**, right? Last time Athena was on Mount Olympus, she turned Medusa to stone. Plus, Athena's a goddess, so she's got powers. In fact, Hestia asked me to fly that key to her so she could free you."

They'd reached the bottom of the hill. Heracles looked at Athena with new interest. "A goddess, huh? Okay, let's go. Circe's palace is this way." He pointed to a second hill up ahead and began to walk faster.

Athena dashed after him. It had been nice of Yellow Wing to say that stuff. She just hoped she *could* help Heracles. She didn't really know much about her goddess powers yet!

"Tell me more about Circe," she said as they hurried up the new hill.

"I've heard she has eleven faces," Heracles said. "And each face has an expression to match its **personality**. She blinks to shift from one face to another."

Strange, thought Athena. But

then many things were strange on magical Mount Olympus. And this island couldn't be far from there, she guessed.

At the bottom of the hill they came to a valley with fruit trees and green fields. Athena and Heracles munched on apples. Yum! Luckily the trees weren't enchanted and rude like some Athena had met on her Mount Olympus adventure. They'd been troublemakers, and stingy with their fruit.

Finally, they reached Circe's

palace at the far end of the valley. Surrounded by beautiful gardens and fountains, the building had a tall tower at each of its four corners.

They knocked at the palace door, but got no reply. Then Athena noticed a sign. She read it aloud. "No entry. Try the door that is left."

They looked left, but there was

no door there. Then Yellow Wing looked right. He pointed a claw. **"*There's* a door!"**

Heracles grinned as they walked over to it. "Circe must not know her left from her right."

Athena grinned back at him. "Or maybe she really did mean the door that is left. The only door *left* to get into the palace, that is!"

"Right," agreed Heracles. They both laughed.

Heracles knocked on the new door.

"Is Circe here?" Athena asked the guard who opened it.

His eyes went from them to Heracles's big club. He frowned. "Did the king send you? Are you planning an attack?"

"Do you think we'd tell you if we were?" Yellow Wing hooted.

"Go away!" yelled the guard. He tried to close the door.

"Wait!" Athena said quickly.

Heracles stuck his club in the doorway to keep it open.

"We're not friends with the king,"

Athena told the guard. "We know he locked up your queen. We're here to ask Circe to help us free her."

Hearing this, the guard looked unsure. "Okay. I'll let Circe decide what to do with you."

Yellow Wing rode on Athena's shoulder as the guard led them inside. They entered a room with walls, floor, and a ceiling made of mirrors! Then he left them there.

The enchantress sat in the middle of the room in a silver chair. She had long black hair and wore a fancy white gown with poufed sleeves. She was **admiring** her **reflection** in the mirrors.

Athena, Heracles, and Yellow Wing went up to her, but still she stared her reflection.

"Um, hello?" said Athena.

Slowly, Circe looked away from

the mirrors. To Athena's surprise, the admiring look on her face spun from sight. A frowny, grumpy face appeared in its place.

"Who are you and why are you here?" the grumpy face asked rudely.

"Uh-oh," Heracles whispered to Athena. He took a step back from Circe, not looking so brave now.

Athena stepped closer. Before she could tell the enchantress about washing up on the island in a boat, Circe went on.

"Never mind. Who cares about you? Let's talk about me." Circe's frowny, grumpy face looked Athena up and down. "I have eleven spinning faces already. Your face is cute and smiley. Adding it will make my collection an even dozen. Come closer, girl."

Athena jerked back her head. "**What? No!** You can't have my face. It's mine!"

Circe's faces spun again, this time stopping on a pouty one. "I don't like your reply," she said.

Athena crossed her arms. "Sorry. But I'm very attached to my face!"

"Fine," said Circe. "Then I'll just lock you in a tower until you agree to give it to me." She cupped her hands around her mouth. "Guards!" she called out. Right away two new guards appeared. **"Wait!"** Athena said quickly. "Hestia sent us here. The queen needs help. Our help *and* yours! Please."

Yellow Wing didn't wait for Circe's reply. The Owlie flew at the guards, claws out. "Whooo do you think you are?" it squawked.

Still more guards appeared. They advanced on Heracles. He swung his club at them. "Get back!" he yelled. "Or I'll knock you over!"

Circe blinked again. This time, a crafty-looking face spun into place. She waved her hands in a magical way at Yellow Wing and Heracles and chanted:

"One, two, three,

Drop to your knee.

Four, five, six,

Grow stiff as sticks."

At once Heracles dropped to one knee and froze stiff. Yellow Wing froze in midair. Then that bird dropped like a large stone on top of Heracles's head. *Thump!* Circe had turned them both into statues!

"Not again!" Athena groaned.

In Athena's last

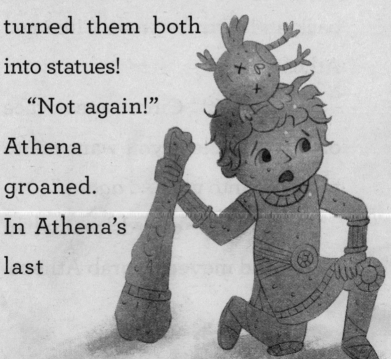

adventure, Medusa had magically zapped some animals into a whole *army* of stone statues!

Circe blinked again. A meanlooking face appeared. She pointed at Athena. "Lock her up!" she shouted to her guards. They looked back and forth between Circe and Athena.

"Snap to it!" Circe's mean face ordered. "Unless you want me to turn you into pigs . . . *again*."

At this, the guards wailed in terror and moved to grab Athena.

"Circe, stop!" Athena yelled. "The queen needs us!" But her voice was muffled by one of the guard's arms. Which made her last words sound like, *"Buh mean sneeze bus!"*

The guards took her to the top of the north tower. There they locked her in a cold stone room. "Please. You have to let me out!" Athena shouted, banging on the door. But the guards were gone.

Athena went to the single high window. It was locked. Even if it hadn't been, the ground was far, far below. Way too far to climb down.

Tears spilled from her eyes. She didn't deserve to be a goddess! She'd failed Hestia and the queen. Not to mention Heracles and Yellow Wing. Feeling sad and tired, she curled up on a stone bench and slept.

4

Visitors

When Athena woke the next morning, she ran to the tower window again. She could see the valley below and the hills and beach and sea beyond. Looking out to sea she noticed something she hadn't seen before. Mount Olympus! Yesterday, it must have been covered in clouds! But today she could see the mountain clearly. She'd guessed right about this island not being far away!

"I wish my winged sandals' magic was working," she whispered. "Then I could magically open this window and fly to Sparkle City. And I could bring Persephone, Aphrodite, and Artemis back to help. Together, we could somehow break Circe's spell on Heracles and Yellow Wing. And maybe even save the queen!"

Just then she heard a sound. *Coo! Coo!* A flock of beautiful white doves was pulling a golden **chariot** across the sky. It was heading her way. And there were three goddesses inside!

A small crown gleamed atop the golden hair of the girl driving the chariot. Aphrodite! Beside her stood a girl with flowers and four-leaf clovers growing in her hair. Persephone! The third girl wore a long black braid and had a bow and **quiver** of arrows slung across her back. Artemis! And she was carrying Oliver in her arms!

The chariot landed between the two palace doors. As her friends hopped down, Athena banged on the window. But no one heard her. Except maybe Oliver.

"Woof! Woof!" He leaped from Artemis's arms, wiggling all over and wagging his tail.

Athena's heart swelled with love as he raced after the girls. They

marched up to the first palace door. Argh! It was the *wrong* one.

Athena saw the three goddess girls read the sign. They looked left before finally spotting the door on the right. She pounded on the window again. At last the girls looked up. Seeing her, they smiled and waved.

"I'm locked in!" Athena shouted down to them. They cupped their ears as if they couldn't quite hear her. "I can't get out!" she shouted.

Persephone nodded to show she understood. "Wait there!" she shouted back.

Ha! Athena thought. Like she had a choice!

Aphrodite knocked on the *right* door. It opened up, and the girls and Oliver entered the palace.

Now Athena began to worry. What would Circe do to her friends? Would she lock them up too? Or try to take their faces? Or turn them into statues like Heracles and Yellow Wing? Back at school, most kids thought she was smart. But a smart girl would have found a way to warn her friends. Instead, she'd only caused trouble. Some goddess she was turning out to be!

Moments later, she heard the sound of a key turning in the door's lock. *Click!*

5

The Big Rescue

Persephone pushed the tower door open. Athena rushed over and they hugged quickly. "Hurry! Let's get out of here," Persephone said.

"How did you get the key?"

Athena asked as they raced down the tower stairs.

Persephone grinned and pointed to the clovers in her hair. "Remember how I used to have bad luck? And then **Zeus** gave me these four-leaf clovers after we got rid of Medusa by turning her to stone? Well, they bring me good luck sometimes. So *luckily*, the key was still stuck in the door." Even though Zeus was about the same age as Athena and her friends, he was a powerful god. He ruled Sparkle City!

"Awesome!" said Athena. The guards must have left the key there after they'd locked her in. "But where are Aphrodite and Artemis?"

"Talking to Circe in that mirrored room," Persephone explained. "For some reason Circe thinks we're spies for the king. But really we came to ask her help to rescue the queen."

"I was trying to do the same!" Silently, Athena wondered if Hestia had sent her friends here because she'd guessed Athena would fail.

Athena and Persephone had reached the bottom of the tower stairs. They entered the mirrored room as Aphrodite said, "For the last time, we are *not* spies!"

Circe was sitting in her silver chair wearing a scared-looking face. She pointed to Artemis's bow and arrows. "Then why does she have those? I know the king sent her to attack me!"

Oliver, who had been sniffing around the Heracles statue, suddenly spotted Athena. "Woof!

Woof!" he barked happily. Wagging his tail, he ran to her. He leaped into her arms and licked her cheek.

"Oh, Oliver. I've missed you too!" Athena said.

Circe blinked, and her mean face spun into place. "So you've escaped, have you?"

Before Athena could answer, Aphrodite and Artemis ran over. The four goddesses did a happy group hug. "Yes, with my friends' help," she told Circe after they broke apart.

"Is that an Owlie on that boy statue's head?" Artemis asked suddenly, pointing.

Athena nodded. "It's Yellow Wing. And that boy is Heracles. Circe turned them to stone, but with a spell, not a Medusa-eye-zap." She looked Circe's mean face square in the eye. "These goddess girls also came here hoping for help in rescuing the queen."

"Whatever," said Circe. "Why should I help? What's in it for me?"

Just then a guard raced into the room. "Hydras! They're coming!" he shouted in terror. **"Run for your lives!"** With that, he zoomed off.

"Too late," Aphrodite whispered, her eyes wide. Sure enough, the girls could hear the monsters breaking down the right-hand palace door!

Persephone glanced out a window. "Look! The guards are sneaking out of the palace through the 'wrong' door."

Artemis frowned. "Those chickens!"

Athena remembered when Artemis used to be afraid of everything—even Oliver! But Zeus had given her a special necklace. Whenever she felt scared, its heart-shaped ruby reminded her that she *did* have a brave heart.

Smash! Bang! Boom!

Circe's scared-looking face spun forward again. "Save me from the Hydras!" she wailed.

"I bet they're working for the king," Athena told her. "Quick! Undo your spell on Heracles and Yellow Wing. Without your guards, we'll need all the help we can get to fight those sea monsters!"

Circe raced to the statues, waved her hands over them, and chanted:

"With these words,
My spell I break.

Both of you,

Will now awake."

"Hoot!" Yellow Wing came to life.
Feathers ruffling, the Owlie hopped
off Heracles's head and flew to the
arm of the silver chair. Club still in
hand, Heracles rose to stand.

"HISSSSS!"

Everyone's eyes flew toward the
sound as all three Hydras crashed
into the room.

6

A Battle

Athena and her friends bravely faced the sea monsters. But Circe, still wearing her scared face, hid behind her chair.

The Hydras stopped in their tracks. Confused, they stared at their reflections in the mirrored room. Slowly their mouths all began to smile.

"Look!" exclaimed the green Hydra. "There are a whole bunch of me and my headsss! I look great!" It grinned at its reflections, its thirteen tongues flicking in and out of its thirteen mouths.

"And I sssee ten of me, each with ten headsss. That'sss a hundred headsss!" the purple Hydra chimed in. "I look awesssome! But how did there get to be ssso many of me?"

"Don't be ssstupid," the red Hydra piped up. "Thossse are only our reflectionsss!"

Though it has only five headsss, er, heads, it seems way smarter than the others, Athena thought.

Heracles frowned at the sea monsters and swung his club to his shoulder. "Leave now and no one will get hurt!"

"*Hisss*" went the Hydras. "We like it here. We're taking over," they sang out together.

"We will dessstroy you!" added

the thirteen green heads.

"In the name of our evil king!" said the ten purple heads. **"You're toast!"** crowed the five red ones.

"Aha! I knew you were on the king's side!" Athena yelled.

As the Hydras advanced into the room, Artemis strung an arrow in her bow. Persephone grabbed a potted plant. Aphrodite grabbed Circe's hairbrush. Athena grabbed two large vases, one in each hand. Oliver growled. Yellow Wing

clacked his beak, ready to peck out the monsters' eyes.

All at once the battle began! The Hydras flicked their tongues and **lunged** at Athena and her friends. *Zzing!* Artemis shot arrow after arrow. Those wiggly Hydras were hard to hit. Sometimes she nicked a tail, sometimes a nose. Often, she missed altogether.

"In the name of the queen, take this!" Athena shouted. She smashed the vases over two of the red Hydra's five heads. *Bop!*

Bop! Bop! Aphrodite thumped its other three heads with Circe's hairbrush. The five heads whirled dizzily. Soon the Hydra looked as tangled as a pretzel!

Meanwhile, Persephone, Yellow Wing, and Oliver fought the ten-headed Hydra. As Yellow Wing clawed and pecked at its purple heads, Persephone bonked them with the flowerpot. (Her good luck kept it from breaking.).

Soon only the biggest, baddest Hydra was left standing. *Bam!*

Heracles batted at its thirteen green heads. They boinged this way and that on their long stretchy necks. Their eyeballs went googly and crossed. Finally, the monster fell over in a heap with the other Hydras.

"Yay, team!" Heracles whooped, waving his club in the air. "We beat them!"

"Look out!" yelled Athena.

"HISSSSSS!" The five-headed Hydra had woken up. It sprang up from the floor toward Heracles.

"You'd make a tasssty treat,"
it said. "But sssadly, my ordersss
are to take you to the king!"

"Oh, no you don't!" someone
shouted. Circe! She wore a fierce
face that Athena had never seen
before as she leaped from behind

her silver chair. Chanting the same spell she'd used on Heracles and Yellow Wing, she turned the red Hydra to stone.

"Couldn't you have done that sooner with all of them?" Aphrodite grumbled. "It would have saved the rest of us a lot of work." But then, seeming to think better of her words, she added, "Thanks for the help, though."

Suddenly, a light began to blink above everyone's head. Hestia!

Soon the tiny, glowing fairylike goddess appeared.

"Well done, all of you!" she said.

"Huh? But what about the queen?" Athena asked in confusion. "I didn't rescue her yet. Didn't you want me to—" She broke off to glance around at the others. Hestia had called on *all* of them to help, she realized. Not just her. Good thing, too. Because it had taken teamwork to get this far.

"I mean didn't you want . . . *us* to rescue her?" she finished.

Hestia laughed a tinkly laugh.

"Even the best of plans can run into wrinkles." She glanced down at the Hydras **conked out** on the floor.

Athena liked that. Not failure, but *wrinkles*. Which, with effort, could always be smoothed out!

"Time to send them back to their lake. Before they have another hissy fit," Hestia said. She clapped her tiny hands together three times. Instantly, the

Hydras vanished. Including the red one, who first changed back from a statue to itself.

Circe's pouty face spun into view. "**Hey!** I wanted to keep that red statue! I was planning to turn it into a fountain with water spouting from all five of its mouths."

"But a monster fountain like that would frighten visitors away," Persephone pointed out.

"Exactly!" Circe said. But then she blinked a smiley face into position. Athena hadn't known she even *had* such a face! "Just kidding! You've proved you're not spies. I'm actually glad you came," she told everyone.

Athena smiled. "You're welcome."

"Now about the queen . . . ," Hestia began, pulling everyone's attention again. "The king has locked her up in his underground palace. His name is King **Hephaestus**. And his palace is below this island's only mountain."

"Some say the king is as powerful

as Zeus," Heracles interrupted her to say. "Besides having magic, he has tons of treasure."

Hestia nodded. "And an army of dwarfs guard his palace. They do whatever he tells them." Just then her light began to blink on and off. **"Oh no!"** said Athena. Hestia was about to disappear!

"Rescuing the queen will not be easy," Hestia continued. "Because—" *Pop!* She was gone.

"Will not be easy because of what?" Athena wondered aloud.

Artemis touched her ruby. "Easy or hard, I'm up for trying." Who's with me?"

"Me!" Aphrodite and Heracles said at the same time.

"Me too. I just hope we aren't under that mountain for too long," said Persephone. She patted her flowered hair. "My flowers need sunlight to stay healthy."

Yellow Wing flew to sit on Athena's shoulder. "Count me in."

"Woof! Woof!" barked Oliver. Which meant he wanted to go too.

Persephone turned toward Circe. "How about you?"

"Um, I'll think about it," answered her scared-looking face.

Now everyone looked at Athena. "You're a long way from home . . . ," Persephone began.

Aphrodite nodded. "We'll understand if you want to go back."

Artemis pointed to Athena's winged sandals. "They can take you home, right? Just like before?"

"Actually, the sandals don't seem to work on this island,"

Athena told them. "So, I can't go home. Not yet, anyway."

But it didn't matter because she wasn't *ready* to return. She'd wanted an adventure, and this one wasn't over. Besides, she'd only just met up with her goddess girl friends again. She wouldn't let them, Hestia, *or* the queen down. No matter how many wrinkles they ran into along the way. That's not what goddess girls did!

"There's no way you're continuing on this quest without me," she said. "If King Hephaestus thinks he can lock up the queen and rule this island, he's got another think coming!"

The other three goddess girls grinned at her. "That's the spirit!" Persephone shouted.

"One for all and all for one!" whooped Aphrodite.

"Yeah, yeah," Circe said, a bored face spinning into place.

Artemis thrust a fist in the air. **"We can *do* this!"**

"All right!" said Heracles.

Athena's heart lifted as she and her friends traded smiles and reached out to squeeze one another's hands. It felt great to be together again. And no matter what troubles lay on the road ahead, together they would stay strong!

Word List

admiring (ad•MY•ring): Liking or approving of something

chariot (CHAIR•ee•ut): A two-wheeled cart drawn by animals (usually horses) in ancient times

clacked (CLACKT): Made a chattering sound

conked out (CONKT OUT): Asleep or unconscious

enchantress (en•CHANT•ress): A woman who practices magic and casts spells

goddess (GOD•ess): A girl or woman

with magic powers in Greek mythology

lunged (LUNJD): Moved forward suddenly

Mount Olympus (MOWNT oh•LIHM•puhs): Tallest mountain in Greece

personality (per•son•AL•ih•tee): A set of emotions that makes someone different from someone else

quiver (QWIV•er): A bag for arrows

reflection (ree•FLEK•shun): Something seen in a mirror

slither (SLIH•thur): To slide and twist like a snake

Questions

1. At several points in the story, Athena worries that she's a terrible goddess and doesn't deserve to be one. Do you agree? Why or why not?

2. What were your feelings about Circe when you first met her in the story? Did your feelings about her change by the end of the book? Why or why not?

3. Why do you think Hestia asked Heracles to help rescue the island's queen?

4. Hestia tells Athena that even the best of plans can run into wrinkles. What wrinkles did Athena run into during this adventure? Can you tell about one time you ran into wrinkles when you tried to do something? How did you deal with them?

5. What adventures do you think might await Athena and her friends as they travel to the palace of the evil king?

Authors' Note

Some of the ideas and characters in the Little Goddess Girls books come from Greek mythology. Athena is the Greek goddess of wisdom and an inventor of many things (including ships, flutes, and clay pots). Persephone is the Greek goddess of plants and flowers. Aphrodite is the goddess of love and beauty. Artemis is the Greek goddess of hunting and animals.

Heracles's Roman name is Hercules. He is the greatest and strongest of the Greek heroes. The famous enchantress

Circe lived on a Greek island. Once, she turned some sailors into pigs (which she threatens to do to the guards in our book)!

We also borrowed a few ideas for this book from the third book in L. Frank Baum's Oz series, *Ozma of Oz*. In that book, as in ours, there is an enchantress. She has a collection of different heads, however, not just spinning faces! And the characters are also on a quest to rescue a queen from an evil king.

We hope you enjoy reading all the Little Goddess Girls books!

—*Joan Holub and Suzanne Williams*